I'm Florally Challenged

Also by
David Colpitts:

The Doggerelist
and other Humorous Poems

ISBN: 978-1-77354-349-9

The Doggerelist STILL
and other Humorous Poems

ISBN: 978-1-77354-380-2

I'm Florally Challenged

(and other (mostly) humorous
tales and poems)

David Colpitts

I'M FLORALLY CHALLENGED
and other (mostly) humorous tales and poems

Published by DWC Publishers, Canmore, Canada

ISBN:
    paperback: 978-1-77354-479-3
       ebook: 978-1-77354-486-1

Publication assistance by

PUBLISHING
PageMaster.ca

Contents

Introduction

This book is for ages 65 and up, with exceptions for precocious 55 year-olds.

If I have no idea what pupper necking is (slowing traffic to look at a cute dog) or Pvris (a rock band, actually), then I'm guessing the under 60s won't know what "dunce cap," "going parking," or "bathroom reader" means, and there is no point in burdening them with what is fast becoming unnecessary clutter of mind and loo.

But where have all the bathroom readers gone? Bathrooms of yore were stocked with well-thumbed short stories and magazines. No longer. "They" say it is bad for you, and not because you are hogging an important seat in a one-holer outhouse. No, since most of us now have multiple bathrooms, it's because extended time on the toilet can lead to hemorrhoids, which can lead to pain, suffering and doctors poking their indelicate nosey fingers into places where the sun don't shine.

And so this small book with its potpourri of short articles and poems has lost what might have been its main readership. Perhaps it could be a bedtime reader, with short articles easily read while one is propped up on a pillow before drifting off, although the idea that it might put people to sleep is hardly what I intended.

Oh, well. It was fun to do.

I live in Alberta and winter in Arizona. This book reflects both locales. I have opted to use American spelling and measurement, not because I wish to go back to the old 36-inch yardstick, even if "metre stick" sounds odd, but because this book will be available in both the US and Canada. Older Canadians will be familiar with imperial measurements, whereas many Americans are not familiar with metric and might think twice about a book of "humour" rather than "humor."

All that's left is for me to say "enjoy," like the waiters in restaurants, but I can't muster their lack of enthusiasm.

But, "enjoy" anyway.

David Colpitts

I'm Florally Challenged

Age creates challenges. You know you're visually challenged, for example, when you can no longer see that grasshopper your five-year-old grandson thrusts to within six inches of your bespectacled eyes. Glasses, contact lenses, lasers and surgery are available to make things look closer, farther, bigger or clearer.

There are other challenges as well, each with its own potent or prosthesis – hearing aids for the auditorily challenged, false teeth for the dentally challenged, hair implants for the follically challenged, wrinkle management creams for the crinkly challenged, Playtex, lycra and latex for the gravity challenged, Metamucil for the regularity challenged, Viagra for the … well, you get the idea.

But what about those of us who are florally challenged? I didn't know I was florally challenged until I joined the Meanderthals – really, that is their name – a seniors hiking group. Every Wednesday from the end of ski season to the beginning of ski season, small groups of Meanderthals trod the trails around Canmore, Alberta, hiking to alpine meadows and along mountain ridges, climbing to cirques and beside glaciers, and bagging peaks.

Bagging flowers, too. One hiker carries a counter to track how many varieties of flowers she sees on a hike, tallying over eighty on a good day. Imagine being able to name that many different kinds of flowers. Meanderthals can name not only those flowers in bloom but also those about to bloom, those not about to bloom and those that have bloomed.

Some Meanderthals, that is. All I could name was the dandelion. But it doesn't count, since it is not a flower but a weed that flowers, unlike the fireweed, which is not a weed but a flower that flowers.

I realized that if I were to become worthy of the name "Meanderthal," I had to learn the names of some flowers. We were catching our breath on a high alpine meadow ringed by snow-topped mountain peaks, where pedals of white and yellow and blue were strewn across a tableau of green, when I confessed I didn't know the name of the flower before me.

Helpfulness sprung from all around. This, I was told by Everybody, was the forget-me-not.

Forget-me-not. Forget-me-not. I concentrated, committing it to memory, stored for instant and accurate recall.

I cast my eyes farther afield. More help came. There was an outpouring of names in Latin, English words in odd combinations, foreign-sounding words with too many consonants, and adjectives metamorphosed into nouns. I tried to remember the avalanche of names but there were too many. What to do? I focused on the first five names that were not in Latin.

At the next meadow of whites and yellows and blues came another barrage of names, of which I could remember just two. These two names, of course, supplanted the first five. At the third meadow, I clung to but one name. My head was nomen-clatured-up, dizzy with labels like butter belles, paint cups and blue brushes. The only flower I could remember for sure was the don't-forget-me's.

David Colpitts

Would mnemonics help the florally challenged? Mnemonics are tricks that help people like me remember things. When you hear a name, for example, you associate the name with something else that is easier to recall. If Bill is introduced to you, you imagine him with a duck's bill on his face. The next time you see him, you remember the bill on his face, which triggers the recall of his name, Bill. Not Donald. Definitely not Daffy.

If mnemonics work for people, they might work for flowers. After all, flowers and girls share many names, like lily, violet, sweet pea and Susan with different-colored eyes. And if it's not a girl's name, it might at least be feminine, like belle or lady slipper. Exclude goldenrod, though, which sounds like a prize for catching a big fish, or a car with too much engine and too little muffler, or the member of a member of a blue movie cast.

I don't know any women with those names except a Susan, and she has the eyes of a chameleon which change color with flavor-of-the-day contacts and in proportion to the number of cocktails consumed. Okay, forget mnemonics.

Two hikes ago, I devised a new tactic. I would concentrate on recognizing the first flower named. I would close my ears to any further names and spend the rest of the hike focusing on that one name. It was a brown-eyed Susan. By the end of the year, I figured my repertoire would include a dozen flowers including those never-forget-ums.

I continued my tactic on the very next hike. Limit: one flower per hike. It seemed to work last time. After all, I now knew that brown Susan-eyed flower besides those unforgetables, and I knew them well. Me, I have total recall of everything I remember.

And on the very next hike, at the very first alpine meadow and the very first flowers, I saw a likely looking candidate. It was small, pretty and blue. I asked what it was. It was a forget-me-not.

Hmmm.

If mnemonics don't work, try animals. There are advantages to learning the names of the furry creatures of woods and fields. There aren't very many. Nor do they hang around waiting for people to identify them. They skitter away at the sound of clicks on a counter.

With animals, I will have to prove my skill at identification only once or twice a hike, if that. And people don't seem to care about the whole name. They're happy to say wolf or bear or squirrel, not flying wolf, timber bear or grizzly squirrel. Heck, it's a whole lot easier. They'll never know I'm florally challenged.

Besides, whoever heard of a person who was faunally challenged?

The Dentist Visit

Brush, floss and visit your dentist regularly.

You might think that regularly means once every ten years, but that isn't the dentist's view. No, he wants to see you every year for a checkup and then again for umpty-ump times for tooth repair, removal or cleaning.

You know when it's time to see the dentist when you get a notice in the mail. The notice is friendly and kind. It's like getting a notice for a tax audit, with more of a "come into my parlor, said the spider to the fly" approach. It creates dread, fear and the sudden realization that you should have been doing something sooner. Like flossing.

I got my notice and phoned the dentist's office. The receptionist always exudes a bright and cheerful voice, hiding the sound of any pain or suffering behind her. Yes, I could have an appointment in two weeks.

Two weeks. I marked it on my calendar and checked – yep, I found barely used floss deep in the recesses of the bathroom cabinet. And, oh joy, floss does not come with a best-before date. The plan was to begin flossing that very evening before bed. Surely two weeks should be enough time to get my flossing up to scratch and avoid The Lecture.

The next day, I got a call from the dentist's office. They had just had a cancellation. Could I come in that very afternoon? Unfortunately, I could. Another major disadvantage to being retired, right up there with Metamucil, prune juice and colonoscopies.

Then off to the dentist, remembering to clean my teeth before leaving the house. Why clean something you're going to get cleaned by a pro who is a lot better at it than you? Probably for the same reason people clean their houses before the cleaning lady arrives.

You arrive at the appointed time, fully aware that your appointed time is not the dentist's appointed time. So you get to sit in the waiting room. It, too, is bright and cheery, with free water at a water cooler. Free water! About the only thing you won't have to pay for in the office.

While you wait, other patients come out after seeing the dentist. They stand before the receptionist with half-frozen faces, get a bill and hand over credit cards. And surprise – no yelp, the type of yelp one makes as one senses one's money bolting for freedom.

There are magazines to look at while you wait. These are not magazines for ordinary folk. No, these are about high-end houses decorated by high-end decorators and filled with high-end furniture and paintings the like of which only appear in museums. Then there are magazines about people, movie stars, royals and such who can afford those high-end houses. These magazines also have articles about who's marrying whom, who's divorcing, who's been running around with so-and-so's ex, and who has just been let out of, let in to or was just visiting a spiffy rehab resort disguised as a clinic. They also have articles on how to improve relationships. Given their divorce rate, the movie stars don't spend much time reading those articles. That's not to mention all those articles about better sex, not of much use to someone barely trying to avoid having the rest of his teeth removed.

Eventually, I get to see the tooth-cleaning lady. She scritched and scratched at my teeth for a while. Then, as expected, came The Lecture about how to brush and how to floss. Basically the same as in grade three, but with your very own personal teacher. That makes it much harder to pretend it doesn't apply to you.

I was given a small mirror to look into my mouth while she pointed out areas that needed *More Work*. I uh-hunned as best I could given the number of latex-clad fingers and sharp metal objects encumbering my tongue. I did my best to keep my most attentive expression on my face, the one of Earnest Interest and Keen Learning. It's a tough expression to master, and even tougher when your esthetics of good taste are being bombarded by latex of bad taste. I had worn that face for years just before the arrival of Santa Claus. I was out of practice. Indeed, I had almost forgotten how to do it, but I'm sure it shortened The Lecture by at least four minutes.

Then the dentist himself appeared, took a look in my mouth, did some more scritching with his pointy metal thingy, and made a comment about changing the cap on my right front tooth – for cosmetic reasons, he said.

I wasn't sure about changing it for cosmetic reasons. At my age, beauty is no longer an option. Instead, I've been working on character, enhanced by a slightly chipped worn front tooth of the sort only Snaggletooth would be proud. Besides, the cap had been there for years. It still functioned well in the event of apples, cobs of corn and fingernails.

He also said something about wanting to holiday in Florida and how expensive it would be. The comments are probably not connected.

He said he understood my attachment to my current tooth and indicated his front teeth which, like mine, could use some cosmetic work. His wife had been after him to get them gussied up, figuring it would be good for business as he could show his patients how much nicer it would look.

That didn't make sense to me. Instead, I reckoned that if he made sure all the other dentists in town had their teeth done up nice and fancy but left his as they were, it would be even better for his business. Everybody in town would think he was the only dentist who could do that work, meaning he would get even more business. Maybe I saved him oodles of money. Maybe enough for him to go to Florida after all.

And so I left the dentist's office, promising to floss as I backed out the door, and paid the receptionist, proud of how I had suppressed a yelp. I recorded my next appointment in my little book, right along with side notes to ask the dentist to use mint-flavored latex, to crank up my flossing activity at least two weeks before the appointment and to practice my Earnest Interest and Keen Learning look.

Make that a Large-Medium

My barrel chest and washboard stomach have switched places. That phenomenon has changed more than my mating habits. It has changed how wetsuits fit me.

My old suit was past its life expectancy. I needed a new one for white-water canoeing in rivers refrigerated by glacial water. Hypothermia, I've heard, is one of the better ways to go, but could render the dearly departed unsuitable for an open casket and I wanted my mother-in-law to see that I had died with a smile on my face. Clearly, I <u>had</u> to get a new wetsuit.

An internet search showed they were readily available online. The sizing seemed straightforward enough: weight, 155 to 180 pounds, height between 5'9" and 6'0". Medium-large. That's me.

The online catalog showed models steely-of-eye and firm-of-chin looking movie star sleek, muscles distinct beneath the rubberized sheath. With a few clicks of the mouse, that could be me.

Well, not quite me. I would have to practice the steely-eye gaze essential for seeking a route through tricky eddies and currents, just like those canoeists pictured in the wetsuits. The ever-present chiseled chin might be a problem, too, but I did have a few days to bushy up some facial hair to hide my three unchiseled chins.

Next task — steely eyes. A few hours of squinting at the mirror did nothing but make my eye muscles sore. Nor was the internet any help. Looking up how to develop steely eyes did produce something on how to remove eye bags in twenty minutes, promising "the results will surprise you," using raw potatoes, cold tea bags or ice-cold metal spoons. Metal spoons over the eyes was not the steely-eye look I was working toward.

As for restoring multiple rounded chins to one by thickening a beard in but a few days – no luck. Not even close. While there were all sorts of commercial and home remedies to thicken hair, at least hair on top of heads or gracing eyelashes, all took months to show any result. So I resigned to waiting for my new wetsuit in hopes that at least the me below the neck would look the part.

I put the wetsuit on as soon as it arrived and pranced over to the mirror sporting my sub-par steely eyes and inadequately enhanced facial hair. Alas, I did not look sleek. My barrel stomach protruded. Bulges ballooned where muscles should ripple. Folds of floppy flab were in clear relief. The suit was a navel tourniquet.

At least my washboard chest did not show. Above my middle, the wetsuit hung in loose folds. It barely moved when I flexed my pecs and filled my lungs to capacity. No, the chest part of the wetsuit was as shapeless as a nine-year-old Spice Girl fan in full regalia.

The medium-large wetsuit did not account for someone whose body had been rounded by years of fine food. It was designed for someone slim of waist and broad of shoulder like Mr. Clean, not for someone shaped like a church bell with clapper.

The suit only fit at the legs with room for Dolly Parton-sized silicone implants at my chest and a boa constrictor grip on my thorax. It was like super compression underwear, small consolation if I couldn't even use my legs. The problem was the, er, clapper part. If I walked, the wetsuit rode up in a crushing crotch clamp. A slow waddle, legs apart like a three-year-old with wet pants, was the best I could do. Anything else would result in short-term pain and long-term threat to those already declining mating habits mentioned above.

The problem is the meaning of "medium-large." I took it to mean medium on the top, large on the bottom. That is, top-down. But I got something that fit a large upper, medium lower. That is, bottom-up. Obviously, they should have labeled it "large-medium."

There's no doubt the fault lies with the medical profession. You see, if the doctor asks me to strip to the waist, she means I should strip from the top, not from the bottom – that is, top-down. She doesn't expect me to ask whether I should take off my shirt or my pants. I'm expected to know. And I won't ask again – at least not until she has finished poking my body orifices with her doctor's dastardly demon digits.

If it's top-down in the doctor's office, it should be top-down everywhere else, including garment sizing. Doctors know about these things, don't they?

But then again, maybe I shouldn't blame the medical profession too loudly. After all, if I can't get a wetsuit that fits in all the important places, there may come a day when I'll need those folk to cure a high squeaky voice.

The Visit

Now Prattling Pete lived deep in the bush
    In a world of solitude,
Remote from humankind and their brassy,
    Clamorous multitude.

His closest neighbor lived far up stream
    And across the blue-green lake;
Known for his bush skills and hunting might,
    His name was Loquacious Jake.

Loquacious Jake and Prattling Pete
    Had a friendship bona fide;
They shared a love of the outdoor life
    With undeniable pride.

The bush provided all their needs,
    From hooch excelling scotch
To tasty gourmet caribou innards
    And fur-trimmed under gotch.

The snow had gone since last they met
    So Jake arranged a trip,
Down the river to the south
    To renew their fellowship.

He yearned for a traditional chinwag,
	Where ideas could be shared,
Information exchanged, old stories told
	And personal vexes aired.

Loquacious Jake pulled in to shore,
	Greeting Pete in a friendly way;
He offered the outdoorsmen's salutation –
	"So how's it goin', eh?"

Pete pondered the question for a bit,
	Seeking the words to explain;
He wanted to give a full response,
	So he said, "Oh, can't complain."

A comfortable silence filled the air
	As water was boiled for tea;
Warming each to the other's presence,
	In quiet serenity.

Then they engaged in small talk,
	A prelude to an articulate flow.
"Rough weather, huh," Loquacious voiced.
	Spoke Prattling, "At least no snow."

The shadows lengthened as they sat
        Thinking their thoughts profound;
Then came that exchange of critical data,
        For which those on the land are renowned –

"How's the bugs?" Loquacious asked.
        Pete carefully concentrated;
Drawing deep on bush-craft lore,
        "A hell of a lot," he stated.

Pipes were lit to the buzz of the bugs,
        As they relaxed in the light of the moon;
And nature's blues hung long in the air,
        The wails of the Arctic loon.

Then they applied their considerable minds
        To complex issues and intrigue;
Savoring the chance of exchanging views
        With their wise and learned colleague.

With measured voice of full concern,
        Loquacious raised a question
About the world's most pressing affairs
        On which to focus attention –

"What's new in town?" he asked. Said Pete,
    "When next ya go fer grub,
There's a brand new peeler ya gotta see
    At Sassy Fanny's Club."

Now Pete was a warm and gracious host
    And hoped that Jake would stay;
But Jake had fully spoke his mind
    And decided to go his way.

And so Pete waved a fond farewell,
    And as Jake left he thought,
"There goes a fine friend and true,
    But boy, he talks a lot."

***

Now each of us is flawed somehow,
    It's just a human trait;
And many a promising friendship ends
    Because of faults too great.

Some choose their friends for charm or wit,
    Or for a mind so grand;
But the one I chose to be my friend,
    Has faults that I can stand.

Stanley and Marie Take a Hike

A Stanley and Stella Stiplebum Saga

"Maybe you should take Marie for a hike," said Stella.

Stanley groaned. Why did all these surprise announcements come at breakfast time? After all, he had already planned a full day of puttering in the workshop, watching football and sneaking an ogle at the latest clandestine copy of Playboy.

"It will give you a chance to bond with Marie while enjoying the fresh air and nature."

"I tried bonding with her just last week when I took her fishing. As soon as I put a worm on her hook she bolted for the car threatening to report me to the Society for the Prevention of Cruelty to ATTWAS."

"What on earth is ATTWAS?"

"It's All Things that Wriggle and Squirm. I don't think I'll be able to bond with her. I'm not a mirror."

"You have to admit that it is good exercise," said Stella.

"Yes, but I haven't been hiking for years. Besides, I don't think Marie wants to go hiking."

"Of course she does. She just won't admit it."

Marie came down to breakfast shortly after.

"Dad thinks the two of you should go for a nice hike today," said Stella.

"I don't want to go for a hike," said Marie.

"Your father is *so* looking forward to it. And I'll make a nice lunch for the two of you."

Marie looked at her mother for a hint of sarcasm, then at her father for confirmation. Stanley smiled at her, that smile that says, "Alas and alack, we're trapped."

"Oh, all right," said Marie. She went up to change.

By the time she changed into hiking clothes, gathered her hair into a ponytail and selected lipstick to match her baseball cap of the week, Stanley had gathered gear and supplies.

Marie came down. "Dad, how do I look?"

"Fine," said Stanley.

"You didn't even look," said Marie indignantly. "Mom, how do I look?"

Stella examined Marie – ponytail pulled through the back of her ball cap just so, safari shirt unbuttoned to three milli-gawks above indecency, tights very much living up to their name. "You look fine, dear," she said.

"Ok," said Stanley, "we're all set. Backpacks, lunch and water. You better get some toilet paper."

"Toilet paper? What do I need toilet paper for?" asked Marie.

"There won't be any toilets once we start on the trail."

"No toilets? I'm not going to any wilderness without a toilet."

"There's a pit toilet available at the trailhead. We can use that before we start."

"Pit toilet? Without running water? I bet it doesn't even have a mirror. And what if I have to go before we get back?"

"You just go. Find a place out of sight."

"I can't believe this – we're going into wild, uncivilized boondocks. What if we meet a bear?"

"I have some bear spray."

"You mean we might *actually* meet a bear? Shouldn't we have a gun?"

"They say bear spray is more effective than guns. I'll also have some mosquito repellant."

"Bears, now mosquitos." Marie looked wildly about her. She didn't see any way to escape. "I don't use mosquito repellant. It literally putrefies my perfume."

"Well, don't put it on. There probably won't be any mosquitos."

"But there might be some."

"Yes."

"And bears."

"Yes."

"Mom, do I *have* to go?"

"Yes, dear. In any case, it's safer if there is more than one on a hike. Safety in numbers, they always say."

"How can it be safer? If there are two of us, twice as many things can go wrong. I don't want to go."

"Now, dear, this is important to your father."

Marie resigned herself to going and did a quick check – phone in case of texts, lunch in case of hunger and peek-a-boo bra in case of cute guys. "Ok," she said, "I guess I'm ready."

The drive to the trailhead didn't take long. Once there, Marie checked her hair, lipstick and eyebrows in the car mirror, adjusted her shirt for maximum effect and made a beeline for the pit toilet.

And came right back.

"It smells," she said, wrinkling her nose. "It's gross, gross, gross. How do they expect anyone to use it? It's called a pit toilet because it's the pits. You'll never, ever, get me inside one of those again. It's yuckier than a swarming slew of slimy slugs. Let's go home."

A car pulled into the parking space four cars down and three young men and a young woman got out. They put on backpacks, the men casting furtive glances toward Marie. Stanley scowled. Marie preened.

One of the men asked, "Are you doing the Itchy Springs Trail?"

"Yes," replied Stanley.

"We'll see along the way," and the four were off.

That's all the encouragement Marie needed. "Ok, we can go." She set off behind them with newfound enthusiasm.

Her burst of energy didn't last long. When she lost sight of the others, she slowed down. That suited Stanley, whose exercise routine consisted of getting in and out of golf carts, pushing a lawnmower around the yard and puffing upstairs with an urgency caused by poor foresight when the main floor bathroom was occupied.

They were all of 19 minutes into the hike when the first mosquito buzzed Marie. She slapped the back of her neck. She missed. The mosquito returned to the attack. Flailing arms failed to discourage it.

"Let's go home," said Marie.

"But we've just started," said Stanley.

"I want to go home. All we've done is walk. I thought we were supposed to hike."

"All hiking is walking but not all walking is hiking," said Stanley. "When the trail starts up the mountain we'll get great views down into the valley – that's more like hiking."

"I don't care. If I want to see mountains and valleys, I can Google them. I'm going home. I can't stand all these mosquitos."

"Just one little mosquito. Do you want some repellant?"

"No way. Not unless its smells like Chanel number 47 or something."

Just then, another foursome of three young men and a young woman with large packs passed them on their way back to the trailhead. Stanley greeted them with a customary "good morning" while Marie feigned a lack of interest. As soon as they passed, she turned and watched them go, taking in the men's toned legs, trim waists and broad shoulders.

"Ok, I'm going home now," said Marie and started back. She was well along the trail before Stanley realized what was happening. He could do nothing but follow.

They arrived at their car soon after and found the foursome's car beside theirs. They were unloading their packs.

"How long have you been out?" asked Stanley, assuming from their large packs that they had been overnighting at one of the backcountry campsites.

"Two nights. We did the Trickle Falls to Itchy Spring Loop Trail. Have you done it?'

It was a question of courtesy only, given Stanley's pudgy belly.

"No," said Stanley, "but it's, um, on my list."

"Great hike. You'll like it."

"Those packs – they look heavy," said Marie. She was less interested in the packs than the physical specimens that carried them.

"Not very heavy – about 35 pounds."

"Oh, that's not too bad. My dad and I are planning to do that very hike soon, aren't we, Dad."

Stanley nodded numbly.

They were on their way home when Marie asked, "Do they have bathrooms at the backcountry campsites."

"Just pit toilets."

Marie recalled the two foursomes they had seen, each with three men and one woman. She recalculated. The odds looked good and the goods looked *great*.

"No problem," she said. "I'm good with pit toilets."

I'm No Longer a Dirty Old Man

Young women are the unfriendliest people in town. Hereabouts it's common courtesy to nod and say "Hi" to those you pass on the streets. Everybody does it except folks visiting from big cities and young women.

I can understand the visitors. They come to town knowing they don't know anybody, but not being from such a friendly place, don't know any better. I try to teach them more respectable manners. When I meet one, I look at them, maybe make eye contact if they happen to glance my way and then at just the right distance I say, "Good morning." That startles them and if it doesn't startle them too much, they'll stammer out some response, like, "Oh, uh, hi." I don't know if it helps, but maybe next time they meet one of us, they'll be more sociable.

But there is no excuse for those young women from town. When you meet them, they take no notice of you. Not just pass by, but pass by like you don't exist.

They use one of three tactics, these young ladies. Tactic number one: her head is tilted down slightly, eyes fixed 4.37 paces ahead on the sidewalk in front of her. Upon her face is a Mona Lisa smile.

Tactic number two: the young lady looks straight ahead, eyes focused on that lighthouse 100 leagues offshore. Her face is set in stone, serious and cold. My bet is she would have to wash her shoes after getting home every day. If you're looking at lighthouses, you can't avoid all that bubble gum, ice cream or brown stuff.

David Colpitts

Tactic number three: this is the more modern tactic. She is mesmerized by her device. Maybe her thumbs are moving at warp speed, brows creased in concentration. She's oblivious to lighthouses, but she might see any brown stuff on the sidewalk and just might miss walking into you.

Or maybe she has the phone jammed up against her ear, her free hand waving about as snatches of conversation float through the air – "No, like, really? That's totally gross." Likely as not, she'll be waving a free arm. You have to be careful when you pass her or you'll get side-swiped. Just time it like passing a lawn sprinkler and you'll be fine.

Some time ago, I passed a young lady who was using tactic number two – that's the "I stare at lighthouses" approach. I said "Hi" – I'm trying to train them, too, just like the visitors. But unlike visitors, she passed on with nary a response. Not a twitch. Not even a blink. Was she deaf?

But it wasn't more than a day later, I went into a store and there was this same young woman behind the counter. Now I was greeted with a smile and a warm welcome. She couldn't have been more helpful. Hard to believe this warm, friendly, young lady had been the same lighthouse-transfixed one from the day before. No, she wasn't deaf.

Apparently, attractive women can be bad for a guy's heart. A study some time ago conducted by scientists from the University of Valencia in Spain found that a woman can raise the levels of cortisol in a man. That's the stress hormone linked to heart disease. Could it be they are actually trying to be kind and helpful by not raising my stress levels? Sounds farfetched.

So I asked my niece, Jan, about this phenomenon. She should know all about the quirks of young women since she is one. Of course, I mentioned that I was sure she would never pass anybody without saying "hi."

Surprise – that's exactly what she would do. She said that if women looked at men as they passed, the men would misinterpret it and assume they could make a further advance – "come on to them" was the phrase she used.

But surely not me. I pointed out I was old enough to be their father or maybe their grandfather.

"Well," she said, "you might be a dirty old man."

Me? At my age? Very hard to believe.

Fast forward a few months. I had been away over the winter and returned home. Walking down the street that first day, I encountered a young lady and, reverting to training mode, said "Hello." She looked at me, smiled and said "Hi." What a beautiful smile. The sun shone brighter, the birds sang ever so sweetly, spring sprung into my step and my heart skipped a beat. What a delight a beautiful smile can be.

Not long after, I encountered another young lady and said my customary "Good morning." Lo and behold, another smile and a "Hi" in return. The sun shone even brighter, more birds sang ever so sweetly, spring sprung into both my steps and flowers bloomed. My chest involuntarily swelled, my stomach tried to shrink, my love handles jiggled and my heart skipped two beats. TWO beats. Then I went straight home. At my age, you don't want your heart missing too many beats. That, and the sudden infusion of cortisol.

Why, with their power to make a guy's day, should these young women withhold their dazzling smiles? Back to Jan for consultation.

"You are getting older, you know," she said.

"Yes," I said, "but not that much older – only a few months." That's when I had this terrible thought, "You mean, they think that now I am too old to be a dirty old man?"

She looked me up and down. She tried to be delicate. "Well, let's face it," she said, "they can tell that you are getting to the age where your love handles are evolving into vestigial organs."

Sigh.

But at least all those smiles are worth it – almost.

My First Hearing Aid

Lawyers tell you when you need hearing aids, right? At least, that's what happened to me some 30 years ago. Of course, my wife had complained for years about my hearing, but I was afflicted with "chronic wife-induced selective hearing syndrome" so didn't pay attention.

The lawyer in question was a pensions advocate, a lawyer working for Veterans Affairs Canada (VAC) to provide legal advice for military veterans who might have a disability arising from past military service. We had served together years before when we both were in the army. He had come to Yellowknife in Canada's Northwest Territories where I was then living to make a presentation to the Legion. I invited him for dinner and later that evening he told me I had a hearing loss. I disagreed with him, but he pointed out I had been in the infantry in the sixties and seventies where frequent and prolonged exposure to weapons firing with inadequate hearing protection made it almost certain I had a pensionable hearing loss.

He was right, of course. After testing by an audiologist and a submission to Veterans Affairs, I became eligible for a small disability pension and free hearing aids. So a simple dinner invitation turned into some beer money.

My hearing aid story doesn't end there.

In due course, my new hearing aids arrived. One did not fit and had to be sent back for re-sizing. I decided to find out if my wife would notice any change in my hearing. I wore my one hearing aid that first day without telling her I had it. She didn't notice any change in my hearing. That night I covertly turned it off, took it out and hid it in a bedside drawer. The same thing happened the next day, and again no reaction.

On the third night, I took it out but failed to turn it off before putting it in a drawer. I didn't know that hearing aids squealed when removed from ears. Nor could I hear it squeal when I wasn't wearing a hearing aid. I only learned it would squeal when my second hearing aid arrived some weeks later.

I could not hear the squeal, but my wife could. She sat up abruptly in bed and asked if I had my new hearing aids. My secret was out – after three days. The squeal did it, not my newfound ability to hear.

I now enjoy an occasional VAC-sponsored beer and appreciate my free hearing aids. I have also learned that "chronic wife-induced selective hearing syndrome" is incurable.

My Hearing Aids Misbehave in Public

Conversations all around me hiccupped when I changed a dead hearing aid battery at a dinner party. It doesn't help that hearing aids look like emaciated translucent maggots. It doesn't help that hearing aids which have been freshly extracted from their ear-hole home look like emaciated translucent maggots with tinges of jaundice. Only ten-year-old boys are fascinated by such things.

I tried to be discreet when I changed the battery, but everybody noticed. The woman on my left suddenly became engrossed – sorry about the word – in the paint on the far wall. The couple across the table sprouted instantaneous invisible blinkers and scrutinized each other's eyes with the sort of passion only shown by eyelash aficionados. The lady on my right locked the fellow on her right in a riveting discussion on how to clean spittoons.

What are you supposed to do when your hearing aid battery quits in public? Do you slink off to a washroom to replace it in private? You might leave the dinner table just as your hostess is serving her Famous Baked Alaska and you'll miss the fireworks. It's a judgment call. Is the ability to hear during the dessert course that important? Or should you stay to see the display of flickering flames contributing to global warming by consuming perfectly good cognac? Your hostess might subscribe to the etiquette that once seated at the dinner table you must remain so throughout – to do otherwise would ruin The Whole Party.

Another alternative is to stay put while you attempt to discern meaningful words through a malfunctioning hearing aid. You strain to listen, swiveling your good ear – the one with the still-functioning hearing aid – to aim in the right direction like a rotating radar antenna. But few people can turn their heads like owls. So you repeatedly ask whoever you're chatting with to repeat herself, first to the point of irritation, then to the point of exasperation and finally to the point of hoarseness. You lean closer to catch more words, a technique of limited success and maximum exposure to garlic breath. If the person you are leaning close to is an attractive young lady, the resultant view of more plunge than neckline has its own dangers.

Of course, you can try to fake it, pretending to hear when you can't. You arm yourself with a phrase book's worth of inane utterances. Phrases like, "Jolly good," "Really?" and "My, how interesting." The goal is to pick expressions that won't get you into trouble or debt. You nod every half minute, occasionally interjecting one of your chosen phrases. The trick is to pick the right phrase. It's all a matter of timing. A sudden bank-breaking vacation to Hawaii taught me that "yes" is not a word to be thrown about when you don't know where it will land. Saying "Jolly good" to your hostess when she informs you that her beloved Fifi just died doesn't lead to repeat invitations.

So, what does the audio-challenged one do? All the options have drawbacks. I sought professional guidance. I asked my audiologist. She suggested that I could change the batteries before going out. Aha, the perfect solution. Except it doesn't work. You see, hearing aids are like children. It's their nature to misbehave in public.

I then asked her what she would do if her hearing aid battery conked out at a State Dinner. She said she would change the battery right there, at the dinner table. Discreetly, of course. No faking and no slinking off to the washroom.

Ignoring the fact that she doesn't have a hearing aid and has never been to a state dinner, it sounds like the right advice. But it needs a public relations campaign to sensitize people to the idea that it's quite acceptable to carry out routine maintenance on hearing aids whenever and wherever they need it. If breast-feeding in public has become an acceptable practice, then surely changing a hearing aid battery can be, too. After all, in the range of personal paraphernalia, hearing aids are more like watches, say, than nursing brassieres.

And perhaps the hearing aid manufacturers could help as well. Instead of designing hearing aids that look like emaciated translucent maggots, they could make them more visually appealing. Maybe put some color into them. Decorate them, even. Imagine, horn rims in your ears. Imagine, a whole new marketing idea. Imagine, designer hearing aids. Imagine, a plethora of new styles to keep up with.

Imagine going broke.

Well, forget that idea. All we hearing-aid users have to do is convince the public that emaciated translucent maggots are not disgusting. And perhaps we have a start, the thin edge of the wedge. Those ten-year-old boys will grow up someday.

Watch My Back

You've heard the expression, "watch your back." What about "Watch MY back?" That's today's politicians for you. Every time they make a speech on TV, there's a throng of people behind them. What do these people do, besides watch the back of a head? Well, that depends on the occasion. It seems to me there are three types of occasions, each requiring a different set of back-of-head watchers.

Full disclosure – I'm not one of the back-of-head watchers. Fuller disclosure – I do not intend to ever become one.

You get the first type after an emergency of some sort, maybe a forest fire, a shooting or a huge explosion. People are concerned. The news spotlights the event. Spotlights attract. Try not to think of moths. Nevertheless, the politician swoops into the spotlight.

Now, if you're the politician, you have to look like you're on top of the situation. You're doing everything possible, deploying resources, ordering those who already know what to do what to do. YOU are in charge. After all, if all goes well, you get a bunch of credit and credit means votes. If things go badly, well, there are always some officials. You can blame them.

At the same time, you're exuding just the right amount of sympathy and concern, balanced with resolve and hope. Meaningful Words must be said. This is a challenging moment. You are vulnerable. Indeed, there is no greater challenge for a politician than to stand before a crowd and cameras and say meaningful words when there is no teleprompter.

So you have to look like you're in charge. But you're not. The ones really in charge are the officials, maybe the chief forester whose forest is being burned down, or the rescue coordinator or the boss fireman. And they are standing behind the politician.

They don't want to be there. They've been dragged away from what they should be doing like beating out fires or pulling people from collapsed buildings. But the boss needs backup and they need their jobs, so they're there.

How do they look? Sometimes they fidget, anxious to get back to real work. Maybe they'll cast an eye around the crowd. Unlike other political backdrops, though, they spend little time gazing at the back of the politician's head. Of course, they look serious, as reflects the grim situation. They realize they are in the public eye and are careful not to yawn, cough, scratch, burp or wince if their politician boss says something they hadn't said he could say. But at least they act like real people. Not so campaign supporters who also form political backdrops.

Campaign supporters are the second type of political backdrop. They are behind someone running for election. They're easily identified, mindlessly cheering and smiling, wearing a T-shirt that says "Vote so and so" (one name only – it's easier to spell). They hold up signs that block the views of those behind them. They cheer every utterance to jam a 15-minute speech of pointless political platitudes into 45 minutes. They learned that from TV, where commercials are inserted to allow a 20-minute program to stretch a full hour. These people don't have to hear or

David Colpitts

think. Everything their chosen politician says is cheered enthusiastically. There's no "huh?" moment – did he or she really say that? Nope, it's all truth and light and sweetness, worthy of wild cheering. Example:

Politician: We need change.

Enthusiastic crowd: Yea, hurray and loud cheer. Wave signs.

Politician: I can deliver real change.

Enthusiastic crowd: Yea, hurray and loud cheer. Wave signs.

Politician: Elect me for leadership.

Enthusiastic crowd: Yea, hurray and loud cheer. Wave signs.

Politician: Elect me for real leadership.

Enthusiastic crowd: Yea, hurray and loud cheer. Wave signs.

Politician: Yakkety yak.

Enthusiastic crowd: Repeat yea, hurray and loud cheer. Wave signs.

The rest of us: Tune out.

Who are these people? Where do they come from? Maybe they're recycled sports fans. Sports fans are fanatical in support of their team, good, mediocre or everlasting cellar crawlers. They know how to holler "yea" and "hurray." Loud cheers are already part of their repertoire. They wear T-shirts or hats showing their loyalty when they go to the stadium. Mind you, some paint their faces, a practice not yet found in the political arena. Not many fans wave signs, but that can't be too hard to learn, can it? On the other hand, campaign backdrop people aren't fueled by hot dogs and beer. That might turn off many of the sports fans from going to campaigns. What then?

Well, how about those people who manage to sit through a whole half-hour infomercial? That's not too different from sitting through a whole half-hour of political pontification. After all, in both situations timing is important and content is irrelevant. Besides, they're already well trained, have unremovable smiles with impossibly white teeth and can respond to signs saying "cheer" or "applause."

And finally, there are those occasions when a politician makes an important announcement. That requires the third type of back-of-head watcher. You know it's a serious announcement because it begins with something like, "My Fellow Citizens" instead of "Friends."

Appropriate gravitas is important. Cue the tried and true Practiced Teleprompter Technique. First, look at the teleprompter on right. Keep chin raised to an authoritative, confident, stately and dignified level. Look down nose but not too much. Then insert authoritative, confident, stately and dignified pauses to allow for applause or, in rare cases, to allow for thought, thereby giving the impression of a statement that has meaning and depth and heft. Note that they have to learn to read ahead without moving their lips.

People are arrayed behind him or her. They do not cheer. They look serious, yet interested and even adoring, their eyes locked on the back of the politician's head. These people are amazing, obviously carefully selected. How else could they sit so still? No yawning despite the words pouring forth. No wiggling, no scratching. How do they suppress a sneeze? Who trains them? Is there someone behind the camera with a sign that says, "Stay still. Stay very still. Do not yawn. Suppress your blink rate to a blink every 73 seconds, even though the light is shining right in your eyes. And no sneaking a peek at the teleprompter to read ahead."

I bet they have a job interview. The job interview might go like this:

Interviewer: Tell me about your experiences sitting still.

A hopeful backdrop: Oh, lots. In school, every day. I got to sit very still, no talking, no funny faces. Like, I couldn't even laugh. Mind you, that dunce cap helped a lot. That, and how the teacher kept fiddling with the strap.

Interviewer: Can you keep your face looking interested but serene, still and unemotional.

A hopeful backdrop: Sure can. I've been practicing every Sunday in church, like when the preacher looks straight at me when he talks about hellfire and brimstone. Like he thinks I've been doing all that stuff he talks about it. I haven't half. Honest.

Interviewer: Can you keep your eyes focused on one thing – the back of our great leader's head, without wavering even if what is said is of no consequence, boring or incomprehensible?

A hopeful backdrop: Heck, that's dead easy. I watch a lot of boring or incomprehensible TV. The only time I get up is to go to the loo.

Interviewer: You won't be able to go to the bathroom in this situation. Know that you'll have to be still. Very, very still – no sneezing or coughing. And particularly no scratching. Scratching is a real no-no.

A hopeful backdrop: No scratching?

Interviewer: No scratching.

A hopeful backdrop: Umm – ok.

Interviewer: Do you have any questions for me?

A hopeful backdrop: I can handle all that. But this is a tough job. How much am I going to be paid?

Interviewer: There is no pay. You have been carefully selected as a person who looks like what people who vote for the party think they look like, though we'll ask you to wear a baseball cap over the orange spiked hair and long sleeves over the tattoo of Cutesy Pie. You follow the nonsense blindly for the honor and glory of the party and the enrichment of those who can get away with it. Just think, your friends will be able to see you on TV, basking in the magnificence of our illustrious leader.

A hopeful backdrop: What's that mean, illustrious?

Interviewer: It means peerless, consummate.

A hopeful backdrop: What's peerless?

Interviewer: It doesn't matter. Actually, it doesn't mean anything – we're talking about politicians, you know. Any other questions?

A hopeful backdrop: Can I claim expenses?

Interviewer: Expenses? What expenses?

A hopeful backdrop: Well, I'm gonna need earplugs, adult diapers, flea powder and a dunce cap.

David Colpitts

Après the Eye Exam

Doctors get your money and they get your goat. If you visit a member of the medical profession, it's going to get worse before it gets better. For me, there's nothing routine about a routine examination. For examinations, doctors are equipped with an array of cold steel tools fresh from the refrigerator, lighted scopes to peer into dark corners, percussion instruments to make you twitch and demon digits to probe your most hidden recesses. Patients are unarmed. And there is nothing you can do about it, short of finding a doctor with small fingers.

My latest eye exam is an example. You'd think, given the number of eye appointments I've had, I'd be used to them, but not so. Each one is torture. I prepared for my ordeal with care, loading my pockets with credit cards, checks, money and a list of twenty questions. I scrubbed my eyelashes and put on my most woeful expression, which said, I hoped, "Be gentle – I'm a wimp."

But I left my sunglasses in the car.

The appointment went as well as expected, which is to say, not well. The attractive assistant pries open my eyes, puts one foot on the lower lid and one on the upper, and pours gallons of unnamed liquids into my eyes until they sting, dilate and ooze yellow.

Reading becomes impossible. Light hurts.

Next, we play Guess the Letters. She wants to know which letters I can read on the eye chart at 20 feet. The same chart was used for my first eye exam sixty years ago. You'd think I'd have it memorized by now. But no, all I remember is the big "E" on top and the third line down, "T O Z." It's a good thing my eye doctor and my memory doctor don't talk to each other.

The letters get smaller and smaller and blurrier and blurrier from top to bottom until I couldn't even guess what they might be. When I can't read any more letters, she prods my naked eyeball with a pressure monitor. This is supposed to tell her if I'm inflated too much.

Then she flashes a light into my eyes and peers with an intensity I haven't seen since my first kiss. The purpose of all this is to prepare me for The Doctor. Softening up, I think it's called.

She asks me to wait for the doctor. This gives me time to think about what might happen next. In football terms, it is known as "icing the placekicker." It is no doubt part of the softening-up process.

By now, I'm really softened up. The Doctor appears. Doctors carry bigger lights to flash into my eyes. Doctors can also be recognized by what they say, which is "hmmm." He can both flash and hmmm at the same time. He leaves. His assistant marks my chart. Actually, it's her chart, since she doesn't let me see it and if she did, I couldn't have read it in any case. Then his assistant – she used to be attractive a few minutes ago, but now she is fuzzy and double – says I can go.

Go? Go where? When I came for my appointment, I could see. Now I can't see, and she wants me to go.

I go down the elevator, along the hall, and through the doors to the outside. It's bright. The light hits me like lightning in a closet. My eyes tear and close tighter than a lady clam rejecting

David Colpitts

an unwanted suitor. I shade my eyes with my hand and open one eye a milli-micro inch for a quick blurry peak. It slams shut faster than a grade 4 student's book at the clang of a recess bell. I try the other eye.

I'm parked somewhere in the middle of the lot. I head off in the general direction, alternately opening one eye, then the other. From the door to the sidewalk. From the sidewalk to the crosswalk. From the crosswalk to the parking lot. From the parking lot to section D. It's like going from the ocean to the beach to my towel wearing an itsy bitsy teenie weenie yellow polka dot bikini, and being blind to boot.

I feel my way along rows of cars to where my car might be. It isn't. Instead, a low-slung sporty car puts on its very own security voice to inform me that I am too close. It sounds like a first date whose voice dropped from soprano to bass.

Where could my car be? I fish my remote car entry from my pocket and push "lock." My car says "beep." It's not too far away. I push again. "Beep," it says.

"What do you think you're doing," says an annoyed someone, invisible through blurry eyes.

Finally, I find my car. Thank goodness for the remote entry. I could never have opened the lock otherwise. Find sunglasses. Find baseball cap. They help, but not much. There's no way I can drive.

It's a chore to blink my way to the nearby mall. The mall has sprouted skylights. Why can't they pull the shades? Don't they know there are people with eye-dropped eyes around here?

I find the darkest corner of the food mall and down enough coffee to keep the whole freshman class awake during a medieval history lecture. Then I slink blindly around shadowy passages, unable to face another coffee, unable to visit stores for fear of bumping into shelves labeled, "you break, you pay," when a horrifying thought strikes. What if I encounter someone I know?

I wouldn't be able to recognize them, not with all that light around. Of course, I wouldn't recognize them in the dark, either. What if they said hello and I didn't know who they were? Oh, the embarrassment of it all. Why don't they rent out a seeing-eye dog or a white cane for a few hours to help people like me?

The doctors' motto is "do no harm." Maybe the doctor didn't think he'd done any permanent harm, but then, collateral damage isn't in their vocabulary.

So if any of you saw somebody like me blundering around the mall last week, hardly able to see, it was me. And I apologize for not recognizing you.

David Colpitts

Hi There

"Hi there," I say.

I confess that I don't know anybody whose name is "There." But I couldn't remember her name, although we've met at countless conferences over the years. And because her name tag had been placed "just there," I couldn't look at it without appearing to look at them.

My memory aside, there are two problems here. One is the failure to print name tags in large enough letters so that my declining eyesight can read them at a glance. And read them at a glance is what I'm supposed to do. You're not supposed to stare at name tags – particularly name tags worn mid-chest by women. That, of course, is the second problem.

You see, name tags are to be glanced at, not admired or discussed. You don't see anybody coming up and saying, "My, what a nice name tag you're wearing today," do you? Even when your glancers are no longer able to glance the glance they used to glance, you're not supposed to actually look at the tags. Your eyes are supposed to take in a jumble of letters by osmosis, decipher them into something meaningful, and, "Hi, Matilda, how nice to see you again."

Should you not be able to figure out the word "Matilda" from a quick glance, you can hardly look more closely, can you? No. Matilda would know right away that you had forgotten her name.

If you do look closely at her name tag, it's worse. She'll suspect that you're staring. At her. At a part of her anatomy. You're just not supposed to stare at things hung at mid-chest if that chest belongs to a woman. Yep, name tags, particularly those that are strung around the neck and hang down to mid-, um, chest, can get a guy into a pile more trouble than leaving the toilet seat up at mother-in-law's.

Now, it's true that women spend all sorts of money to improve the shape, size and view of their cleavage. Garments have been structurally engineered to lift and puff, pout and point, round up and out. When that is not enough, magazine ads tout a plethora of creams and exercisers to enlarge or reduce. Others, too, cash in. Surgeons, anesthetists, medical insurance companies, scalpel sterilizers, silicone researchers, saline solution manufacturers, and, if things fall down, so to speak, lawyers, all make a ton of loot doing what nature didn't do.

Men would spend money to improve women's cleavage, too, if the women didn't do it themselves. The results, after all, speak for themselves. Women have bigger, shapelier busts, designer breasts to fit the fad of the day and fantasy of the night. Without such silicone valleys, Baywatch would never have bounced so high in the ratings.

Despite all the money and attention paid to bosoms, you're still not supposed to stare. Even a man who can no longer see a baseball traveling a mere 82 miles an hour on a 55-inch digital television screen isn't excused. Somehow, you're supposed to notice but not look. You're supposed to notice, but not be noticed noticing.

David Colpitts

Yet, the point of all this effort by the noticee is to be noticed, isn't it? Otherwise, why all the fuss? The noticer, having quite properly noticed without having been seen to notice, is then placed in the predicament of how to express an appropriate level of flattery, if any. It's tough. He can't say, "My, but your bosom is heaving nicely today." About all he can say is, "You look well," or, "I like what you've done with your hair." That's hardly adequate, given the distance between hair and the part of the anatomy in question.

All of which highlights one of the inequalities of this world. Men in polite company can't gaze at a woman's chest. Women, though, can gawk at a man's. Women can even touch a man's chest, to adjust a tie, for example, or brush off lint or straighten a name tag. But you don't see men touching women's chests to brush off lint without getting more than a big brush-off themselves.

If a man can't stare at a feminine chest, even a chest with a name tag positioned "right there," where can he look? Prince Charles was once reported to have remarked, when conversing with a woman sporting a particularly daring cleavage, that his father told him to always look women dressed like that in the eye. Eyes reveal all, it is said. Perhaps, but they don't reveal names. That's not a problem if you're Prince Charles; for the rest of us, there are name tags.

I know I should remember the names of those people at the conferences. I'm not alone, of course, or name tags would never have been invented. But because I can't see them without peering closely, those darn things are of no use. Not unless I stare. Not unless I'm prepared to get into trouble.

Don't get me wrong. If I thought I could get away with it, I would look at the name tag carefully, bend down to bring the name tag to eye level, move closer, read the letters and even study them if pronunciation or spelling might cause difficulty. But no, society tells me that I mustn't gape. And if society doesn't mention it, my wife surely will.

It might help if women's names were shorter and less than two syllables. Men sport names like Matt, Mark, Luke and John. Even when men have longer names, like Richard, they're shortened to Dick unless the men are movie stars or British. Women, though, are called Mary or Celine or Brenda or Cynthia, not Mare or Cell or Bren or Sin. Because their names are longer, they're harder to remember and it takes longer to read their name tags.

Thus, at conferences, I camouflage poor memory and poorer eyesight as best I can, making furtive glances towards bulging sweaters behind fuzzy-lettered name tags, hoping my glances will not be misinterpreted as inappropriate. Or, in cases where surgeons, creams, exercisers, or – dare I say it – nature, have done marvelous work, hoping that my glances will be misinterpreted.

"Hi, There," I say.

"Hi There, Yourself," Matilda says.

Touché.

David Colpitts

Helping in the Kitchen

A Stanley and Stella Stiplebum Saga

Wives respond to husbandly deeds on an escalating scale ranging from a Level I "oh-oh" all the way up to a Level V "oh m'god." Retire, and you can rocket your dear spouse through them all in just a few days.

Stanley figured he could trade years of slaving eight hours a day over a cold desktop, Monday to Friday, to slaving a few minutes every day over a hot stovetop. After all, he thought, why should he spend days chasing a little white ball over carefully manicured grass, entrapping edible wild foodstuffs with hook and line, or risking motion sickness in a hammock when he could help out by taking on more household chores?

He decided to help Stella in the kitchen.

It was a unilateral decision. "Oh-oh," Stella said, invoking a Level I response, which raises the question, can one harm oneself by raising one's right eyebrow halfway to the hairline?

Why not help, he reasoned? After all, he already knew his way around a kitchen. Beer in the fridge, popcorn in the cupboard and microwave above the stove. Heck, he's got two-thirds of it half beat.

"You can tidy up and take the garbage out," Stella said.

Stanley was sure he was no more dirt-blind than most men were. A quick inspection confirmed that the place looked tidy enough already. Nevertheless, he poured out some greasy water from a pot and then hunted for the garbage can. It was under the sink just where he remembered it from last month. There was some sputtering behind him as he took the garbage out, something about chicken stock NOT being greasy water, whatever that meant, but never mind.

"Give me another job. Any job. I can do it," Stanley said.

He was assigned to table setting, all by himself.

That was a lot of work for one day, so he went back to watching cartoons on TV.

His offer of help again the next day was greeted with a whoosh of breath, a typical Level II two response, which raises the question, can one harm oneself by sighing too much?

In the next few days, Stanley mastered garbage removal and table setting, although there were comments about knives on the right and forks on the left. Or was it knives on the left, forks on the right? No matter. He reasoned it was time to graduate to cooking.

"You can't even boil water," was Stella's response.

Aha, something to prove.

First, Stanley opened a bottle of sherry and poured himself a glass. All the best chefs cook with sherry.

Then he found a pot, took a drink of sherry, filled it – the pot – with water, took a drink of sherry, and set it – the pot – on the stove. It didn't take him long to figure out that the left knob turned on the left front burner, the next knob turned on the left rear burner, and so forth, all the way up to four knob/burner combinations. He took a drink of sherry, turned a burner on and congratulated himself on his cleverness. So far so good.

Stanley watched the pot. Nothing happened. He watched some more. Still nothing. Was the burner hot? He poked it with a finger.

By the time he had iced his finger and swaddled it in gauze, there were little bubbles in the pot. Is that boiling? Better wait. Maybe Stella would say it was boiling. He looked over. Still, she said nothing. But that foot-tapping was becoming annoying.

Then the water began to churn, with lots of bubbles. It spattered the stove.

Is this boiling? Must be.

"How long does water have to boil before it is done?" Stanley asked, which raises the question, can one harm oneself if one rolls one's eyes deep into one's eye sockets?

Over the next few days, Stanley was sent back to table setting and garbage removal, skills that he felt had become exceedingly well polished. Time to seek a greater challenge.

"Tonight, I'm going to cook a dish," Stanley announced.

"Not again," she said, invoking a Level III response.

"Look," he said, "I can boil water, so I can cook," which raises the question, can one harm oneself by narrowing one's eyes too much?

"Start me out easy," he said. "Give me something that doesn't have ingredients."

Stella handed him a box of rice. Was a box that small enough to feed us both, he wondered? There were directions on the box, something about adding rice to boiling water. Simple, surely, given that he already knew how to boil water. True artisans didn't need to read directions, so he decided to check them later if required.

However, he wondered if the minister was coming to dinner. While he waited for the water to boil, he checked the calendar. Nope, the minister wasn't coming. Nor was it Sunday. It was like any other day, of no special significance. So why, he thought, was he given *converted* rice to cook?

As soon as the water was boiling, he emptied the box of rice into the pot, which caused a choking sound behind him.

"Get! Out! Of! My! Kitchen!" Stella said, for reasons Stanley didn't understand. But he did understand a Level IV. Which raises the question, can one harm oneself by clenching one's teeth too much?

"I'll set the table," Stanley offered.

"Out!" she said, "OUT!" She followed him all the way to the doghouse.

She turned back into the kitchen. All that could be seen of the pot was the lid teetering on top of a ballooning heap of rice. A volcano of steaming white cascaded from the pot to stove, from stove to floor.

The sound of "Oh m'god," escalating from low alto to glass-breaking soprano broke the sound barrier. It was a leap from Level IV to Level V in an unprecedented seventeen seconds.

Which raises the question: can one harm oneself by golfing, fishing or sleeping too much?

David Colpitts

Bon Courage

The farmer leapt from his truck. He was short, of indeterminate age, with a weather-beaten face, fierce eyebrows and lively, friendly eyes. The whole effect was topped by a beret.

"*Bonjour*," he said.

So began a short conversation in French.

"Were you cold last night?" he asked.

"No, not too cold," I said. It wasn't really a lie. I wasn't TOO cold. I hadn't died from hypothermia.

"How far are you going?"

"To St Jean Pied de Port."

"Bon courage," he said, lifting a callused hand in a clinch and giving a curt nod. He said it the way a coach might encourage his athletes, "Atta boy. You can do it. Keep going." Just that brief conversation and he was off, spurts of dust kicking up behind his rattling truck.

"Bon courage." What a perfect expression. It means be of good courage, be brave, persevere. We don't have anything like it in English. "Good luck" is hardly the equivalent. When people say "good luck," they imply you can't do it all by yourself and there's some chance involved. Not with "bon courage." It's all up to you. It says you can do it, you can deal with whatever challenges come your way and you don't need a four-leaf clover or that rabbit's foot.

I was on day four of a thirty-day walk across southern France, following one of the four historic Chemins de St Jacques that join the medieval pilgrimage route to Santiago de Compostela in Spain, the better known Camino de Santiago. I stayed in hostels or, as on this particular morning, in my tent. I had camped by the side of a narrow farm road. The farmer had driven by my tent at first light when I was still in my summer-weight sleeping bag, wearing everything I owned but boots and eyeglasses.

The clatter of the truck woke me. I got up, the frost still on the ground. To the east, the sun poked up over the horizon, illuminating distant fields bordered by the large rock fences of the Aubrac region. In the opposite direction clustered a dozen tan-colored cows, just three short paces and a strand of wire away, staring at me with unsettling curiosity. The massive Aubrac bull, some distance away, couldn't have cared less. The farmer returned half an hour later when the exchange occurred.

I was still hundreds of miles away from my destination. I was looking forward to a walking-pace journey through rural France, experiencing its history, surprisingly good hostel food and the mobile community of like-minded individuals from different nationalities and backgrounds. Call it soft adventure. Or, better, tough tourism. Along with the enjoyment would come challenges. Not everything would be easy. After all, ahead lay .... Well, who knew at that time, but heat, cold, rain, steep hills, blisters, and sore shoulders would have been a good guess.

I worked through the early morning stiffness brought about by cold hard ground, packed up and ate the last of my bread, cheese and yogurt. Coffee would have helped, but since I planned to stay in hostels most of the time, I hadn't brought a stove. Lack

David Colpitts

of coffee may be a serious situation, but not a grave one. It would be another hour or two before I would find a café. But that morning, I started the day's walk with a lightness of step, "bon courage" echoing in my mind, as it did through the next weeks to my destination.

Bon courage, indeed. The French have had their share of adversity that they have met with courage. As I walked through the many small French villages, I was reminded of the courage of this nation.

War memorials in every town square listed the names of countless citizens who had given their lives for the country. Small villages, with a population of just a few hundred, might have lost dozens in the First World War, fewer in the Second. The inscriptions on the memorials varied somewhat, but would say something like:

La COMMUNE de [name of the village]
A ses ENFANTS
MORTS pour la FRANCE

Translated, it was to the children of (name of the village) who died for France. Then would follow a list of names. Resistance fighters of the Second World War or those who fell in Indo-China or Algeria might have separate memorials or might be included with the others.

Not only were the names inscribed on memorials in the village squares, but in every church or cathedral. There, too, was a wall plaque containing the names of the fallen. So many had the same last name, brothers or cousins, casting a somber spotlight on the multiple sacrifices of but a single family.

France suffered greatly in the two great wars, particularly in the first when over 1.3 million soldiers and sailors lost their lives. After the war, it is estimated that 179,000 war memorials were established, from the simple plaques in churches or modest ones in little villages to the magnificent ones in the large cities or at the sites of the greatest battles.

Could the tremendous valor of the nation have been inspired by that phrase, "bon courage?" I like to think so. It certainly inspired me.

Self-Cleaning Clothes

There are two types of people: those who have to wash their clothes every once in a while and those who don't stink up their clothes. The latter ones are called nudists.

I belong to the first group. That way, I don't embarrass myself with an unsightly body, a body unadorned by rings, diamonds, or pearls placed perilously close to vital body parts or my nipples. Besides, where would I put my car keys?

Washing clothes isn't that easy. It may come naturally to some people like Mr. Clean, but for the likes of me, it's fraught with peril. A simple mistake can color a whiter-than-white white shirt to pink or convert a Sumo wrestler's wool sweater to Twiggy's.

There are labels to tell you how to wash your clothes. Sometimes the labels have symbols. They are meaningless. There are triangles or circles or cups with little waves in them, or what looks like the letter "a" in some exotic font like Franklin Gothic Medium or Leelawadee UI Semilight. To compound the confusion, these symbols can be supplemented with Xs or dots or underlining. Does that mean that the shirt I have with a circle with one dot can only be washed with another shirt with one dot and only one dot? Can I wash it with a two-dot shirt? Or a no-dot shirt?

Next time, I'll only buy clothes without symbols. Socks fit that category since they don't have symbols or words, but I'm pretty sure I'm still supposed to wash them.

I thought I would be able to figure out washing instructions that had only words. "No ironing" is pretty clear. So is "no bleach." But what does "wash with like colors" mean?

It used to be simple. Eons ago, I was told colors needed to be separated from whites. But some whites can be colored. Or is it the other way around? No colored can be white. Or is that the other way around? Now the label says "wash with like colors." Is blue like red? Or gray? And what about striped shirts? They have several colors – which one to use?

Further, some clothes should only be washed in cold water, and that means using specially engineered soap. Those clothes need cold water to keep them from shrinking, unlike me. I shrink if I'm plunged into cold water – actually, parts of me almost disappear, which is another reason why I don't swim at a nudist beach.

Specially engineered soap for cold water? That's only part of it. There are soaps for delicates, soaps for hard water or soft water, soaps with bleach and soaps with phosphates. And then, am I supposed to add fabric softener to make my fluffy soft towel fluffier and softer? Heck, I just want clothes that look vaguely clean and don't smell any more.

Coloreds or whites, cold water or hot, this soap or that, fabric softener not – all this is beyond my domesticality quotient. I used to wear pink socks that were too small. Now all I buy are pink-immune brown socks. They are too small, but they aren't pink.

Washing, of course, is only half the job. Once the clothes are clean, they have to be dried. This should be done before they are worn, which means having more than one pair of socks, a problem if you have a sock-consuming drier. Drying is that feature wherein you discover that clothes that are labeled "perma-press" aren't.

The labels also provide clues on drying. "Tumble dry low," it says. That's confusing too. My drier doesn't have a setting for "tumble dry." I can set it on low or high or somewhere in between, but not "tumble." What if I want to put them out on a clothes rack to let them dry in the sun and breeze – is that allowed? Not if I'm supposed to tumble dry them low.

There are techniques to avoid washing so often. You can wear your shorts or T-shirt for a day, then turn it back to front and wear it another day, remembering, should you be in haste, that the fly isn't readily accessible. The next day, put them on inside out, and finally, on day four, put them on backward and inside out. This will give you four days of wear, recognizing, of course, that you'll only get two days out of a pair of socks or, to make an educated guess, a bra.

You can extend four days to eight. Simply sprinkle laundry powder onto your clothes each morning before you put them on. Remember to check your raincoat for leaks before venturing out in rain or you'll find that your Breeze bubbles, your Tide turns, your Wisk woozes, your foamy Fab froths, your Bounce bounces, or your Surf suds, giving nothing to Cheer about, putting you in a lather, and making you Glad to see Sunlight, er, glad to see sunlight.

Further, you might consider getting another four days by simply replacing laundry powder with industrial-strength rug cleaner. I have a friend who was wondering whether to try it. He's been apprehensive ever since he heard a rumor that a young Howie Mandel once used it to shampoo his hair.

But rug cleaners could have additional benefits, particularly those touted for getting rid of pet hair. After all, bald-headed chests are all the rage. Heck, you would not only trim your bikini line, you would get rid of it altogether, and start another fashion trend at the local nudist beach.

What we need is a major scientific advancement, a leap forward in the fight against filth. Stain-proof pants look promising. You can spill beer and pizza on them, the ads say, and they still look as good as new, but I wouldn't try it with a hot match. If pants can be stain proof, isn't it a short step to becoming dirt proof? And besides, if they are stain proof, how would anybody ever know they are dirty? Ok, so you have to spray them with deodorant once a week, but that's a small price to pay.

Or in another radical approach, someone should invent self-cleaning clothes. Couldn't they apply the same ideas used in self-cleaning ovens to clothes? Just plug them in overnight, and voilà. Don't forget to unplug them before wearing them to avoid getting the electric fence experience without the fence. And now they've come up with self-cleaning windows, and you don't even have to plug them in.

There is one big difference between clothes and windows, though: the window cleaner lobby is not big. The "I Love Laundry Soap" lobby, on the other hand, is huge, rich, and ... clean (so to speak). The washing machine lobby is not far behind. Self-cleaning clothes would put the laundry soap makers and washing machine makers, not to mention that annoying guy in a spotless white suit, out of a job. It would add lobbyists to lists of the unemployed. How many lobbyists? Well, to give a precise figure, oodles. Gone would be political donations of money, free

David Colpitts

meals and yearly supplies of laundry soap to politicians who don't do their own laundry anyway. No longer could they reluctantly accept free trips to view washing machine factories in deprived areas like Macau, Monaco, or Hawaii.

It's clear that self-cleaning clothes won't be coming anytime soon and I better get used to washing my clothes once in a while. In the meantime, I think I will give rug cleaner a try. And I have also been wondering about Draino.

So if a friend calls to ask what I am doing, I don't want to tell him I'm baffled by what should be the simple job of washing clothes. I'll tell him instead that I'm applying a thermal liquid chemical to a range of flexible materials of complex composition under difficult conditions and subject to hitherto undefined and possibly surprising results.

Nature Calls

Why did I not learn everything that I needed to know in kindergarten? After all, that's what the book said – it said you learn everything you need to learn in kindergarten. I didn't. Even the town knew and put a sign on my street to tell the whole blinking world. It said, "Slow Children Playing." So as a result I keep learning new lessons well past kindergarten age and throughout life, and no more so than when hiking or camping.

In the summer, I hike and backcountry camp in the Canadian Rockies. In the winter, I hike in Arizona. Over the two decades I have been hiking, I've learned a heap of things my kindergarten teacher never thought of. Take, for instance, answering the call of nature when in nature and not in the classroom.

In kindergarten, it was easy. You put up your hand, and, provided the teacher hadn't figured out you were trying to skip class, she'd give you permission to leave the room. You then made your way to the washroom with a sign that began with the letter "B" for Boys.

When out in the countryside, though, there are no designated washrooms. You need to consider more things than just the sign on the door. Like wind direction. Face the wrong way on a windy day and the wet on your clothes can't be explained by blaming spray from the sink tap. You also need to check the way the ground slopes so you don't pee up a downslope, for the same reason – there being no sink.

Even though there are no "Bs" or "Gs" in the woods, there are gender preferences. Specifically, the women tell me they do not like areas with high tickly grass.

Men, however, seem to prefer areas with trees or shrubs. They will spread out, facing the tree of choice. If the hike takes them above the tree line, there won't be any trees and maybe no bushes. Answering the call of nature in such a place means more exposure.

You may know "exposure" as a mountaineering term. It refers to empty air above which climbers sometimes find themselves. For hikers, who would only find themselves above empty air by accident, it refers more to the potential hazard of a long fall off, say, a high cliff or from a narrow ledge. Some hikers are comfortable with a degree of exposure, being sure of foot. But not me. I don't like it one bit and will stay well away from the edges of cliffs. Narrow paths just a few feet from a drop-off bother me. High mountain peaks offering 360-degree views from on top of the world can make me nervous. Indeed, I've discovered that the most exposure I can stand is peeing above the tree line.

In kindergarten, going to the bathroom meant going "number one" or "number two." On a hike, number one is easy to deal with. It's number two that calls for more effort. Indeed, Kathleen Meyer, a nature writer, has written a popular book called *How to Shit in the Woods*, now into its fourth edition.

That's a lot of paper to explain a simple process that people have been dealing with for thousands of years. The essentials could be described in a few sentences, namely, bury the, um, product away from a watercourse or campsite, and either bury or carry out any toilet paper. Of course, it's a good idea to bring enough paper and a bag for the used paper if you don't want to put it in your pocket. And it's a really good idea to keep your clothing and boots well out of the way of the action. That's about it, except now, in some parks, for example, you are required to carry it out. And so another lesson – when in such a situation, leave your prunes and Metamucil at home.

And no, the book wasn't printed on soft enough paper, although it might be useful in an emergency. She notes that leaves can also substitute in a pinch and provides guidance on what type of leaves to use. So can lichen, which is what some of the early peoples in North America used. Lichen has the added benefit of having a scrubbing effect. And, clearly, avoid leaves from poison ivy or the itch will be worse than from over-scrubbing.

Obviously, I should have learned these things in kindergarten. The answer – take kindergarten kids out hiking. They'll learn more and maybe somebody will be able to save money by getting rid of those "slow children" signs.

While carrying out this specific function, you will not need a bathroom reader like *How to Shit in the Woods*. For one thing, the position is uncomfortable and therefore unsustainable, and for another, by the time you've read all those instructions, it will be too late.

Oh, and one more thing I learned – those mosquitoes have no sense of decency.

Soccer and Other Games

A Stanley and Stella Stiplebum Saga

Any resemblance, however slight, to any person, living or dead, and particularly living, is meant to seem purely coincidental, unintentional and accidental or, in that technical language so often used by writers – a fluke. Further, all names have been changed to protect the author.

Stanley and Stella Stiplebum's daughter plays sports with the grace of a clumsy sloth. So why on earth would she take up co-ed soccer?

Stella took pains to explain it to Stanley, somewhat more patiently than he felt was warranted. She said Marie hadn't had a social life since she got back from college and she should get out and meet people.

When a woman says she is going to meet "people," she means "men." Even Stanley knew that.

But he had to admit, getting Marie out of the house was a good idea. She was spending far too much time in front of the mirror. Fortunately, mirrors do not wear out with use.

If Marie was going to play soccer, Stanley figured he could help. He dug out his old soccer ball from the basement, hammered two sticks into the lawn to represent goalposts and invited Marie to their first backyard practice session. It was also the last, and it lasted just seventeen and a half minutes.

That's when Stanley told Marie she had to hit the ball with her head. She told him she would do no such thing. She said she would not, repeat, WOULD NOT, put her hair between her head and the ball. She went on about the hours she had spent fixing her hair and she was not about to become bald like Stanley just so she could hit the ball with her head.

Next, he dug up old records of the teams. He might not be able to hone whatever latent soccer talent she had, but he felt he could at least link her with a strong team. He checked wins versus losses, goals for and goals against, and team sponsors.

Team sponsors? You bet. Truth be known, he didn't want her on a team sponsored by Voluptuous Angelina's Late Night Massage Parlor, and a team sponsored by birth control pills would give the wrong idea. The Kinetic Kickers was clearly the best bet.

That weekend, the league was holding its first-of-season organization day at the local soccer pitches. Stanley took Marie with him. Half a dozen teams were forming.

He pointed out the Kinetic Kickers, how well they handled the ball, their clever set plays and strong discipline. In retrospect, "strong discipline" may not have been a selling point for a young woman. Then he said, "But, you can't go wrong with a sponsor like Sudsey's Soapy Shampoo. I bet they even give out free samples."

Marie looked over at the adjoining field. "I'm going with the Nobby Neez," she said.

"The Nobby Neez? Why with them? They had the worst record last year. Besides" (he figured this would be the clincher) "they're sponsored by a family giving away kittens."

"It's the jerseys. The Kinetic Kickers have orange ones and I'm a winter." She fluffed her hair and sighed. "Besides, the Nobby Neez have more cute guys."

"You're a winter? What do you mean, 'winter?'"

"It's my coloring. Winters don't look good in orange."

Stanley pointed out that her coloring was like everybody else's, which was flesh color. That wasn't the right thing to say.

After supper, he complained to Stella about how Marie had scorned his exhaustive and definitive research.

"Marie wants to meet people. Soccer is a good way of figuring everybody out," she said.

"What do you mean, 'figuring everybody out?'" Stanley asked.

"It's a great game for women looking to meet a guy because there's always someone to whistle at you, you can see who knows how to use their heads and you can see which guys are on the ball."

Stanley didn't know what to think of that, but he was sure it was no reason to play soccer. Surely you play for the friendly competition and exercise.

"Boy, it's a good thing we didn't play soccer before getting married. You can't be manipulated with something as simple as softball," was all he said.

Two days later they had a new kitten. Two months later, Marie introduced her parents to Brock, one of the star players of the Nobby Neez. Over supper, Stanley learned the two of them had much in common. They both liked bungee jumping as a spectator sport. Something about screams of terror as people snap their spinal column with an echo like a chiropractor's chortle.

And they both liked odd reality shows, like those that see who can sit the longest on an anthill in the nude.

Even Stella made no comment, a rare event indeed given that there is no woman on earth who can't find fault in a man.

Later, Stanley remarked to Stella that he had enjoyed meeting Brock and how much the two of them had in common. He pointed out, not without a tinge of pride, that psychologists say women tend to marry men who are like their fathers.

"Yes," Stella said. "Now you know why mothers cry at weddings."

Stanley switched the subject. "Why is Marie still playing soccer? She's now found someone and she's so bad at the game. All she does is stand around, and if the ball comes near her, she squeals and flounces out of the way."

"Oh, it's not for her, it's for him."

"Oh, you mean," Stanley said, "that she's sacrificing her interests for his while enjoying a shared activity and warm companionship?"

Stella snorted. "It's because soccer is ideal training for a husband-to-be."

Stanley guessed he could understand that. "You mean it provides exercise while developing teamwork and collaborative achievement?"

"No," she said, "it's because he'll get used to being told when he's out of bounds, he'll get used to being kicked in the shins, and he'll get used to not scoring as often as he wants."

This was alarming news. Poor Brock was being softened up, trained even. Secretly, Stanley resolved to tell him.

"Don't you dare," said Stella.

Stanley put on Innocuous Face, Professional Grade, "Don't I dare what?" he said.

"You know."

How did she know, he wondered? Surely it's not fair to the poor guy not to warn him. But then, something alerted him about their courtship years.

"Years ago, when we were playing softball – you didn't expect me to learn stuff from that, did you?"

She looked at Stanley all wide-eyed innocence. "But dear, what makes you say that?"

He thought back to those days, to secret signs between coaches and players, to unexpected curveballs, and, most of all for a young guy, to how hard it was to get to first base.

Call it an awakening, if you will, 25 years too late.

Stella is right, he decided. He won't tell Brock, for his own good. And Brock's. But tomorrow, the two of them will start boxing lessons. They'll learn footwork so they can dance out of trouble, they'll learn how to roll with the punches and they'll learn to keep their guard up at all times.

Sports are not the only games men can play.

The Sermon

'Twas a foggy day at the vicarage;
    A fog of mind, not sky,
For the fuddle came from holy wine
    Filched early on the sly.

Vicar Victor's tongue was thick,
    His brain a quivering lump;
His bloodshot eyes could barely focus
    On his morning coffee cup.

The Vicar called his preacher friend
    To take the service that day;
The offer of coin coaxed Preacher Jude
    Who was delighted to help for pay.

Now Preacher Jude was older now
    And past his fiery prime;
He'd retired from the pulpit,
    But filled in from time to time.

Jude shooed the moths from his clerical gown
    And starched his collar white;
He scoured his files from decades past
    For a sermon exactly right.

It was his favorite Sunday sermon
From thirty years ago;
Fire and brimstone and message stern,
The lessons apropos.

'Twas fire and brimstone brought to life;
It once so wowed his flock,
They dared not sin for two whole hours,
So thorough was its shock.

He strode up to the pulpit,
Scruff hair o'er running his ears,
Spindly legs in gaudy socks;
Scuffed shoes unshined in years.

His pince-nez was askew upon his nose,
His nose hairs neatly trimmed,
Flaring eyebrows turned up at tips,
His piercing eyes undimmed.

He started by saying how honored he was
To be invited there;
Just a humble substitute
To fill in for Morning Prayer.

He pointed to a broken window,
        Now covered with a board;
An introduction to his theme
        As his eloquence soared.

The board was placed in a time of need;
        Today it's a faded red;
Temporary, but enough for now,
        A fill-in like him, he said.

His open arms included them all
        As of heaven and hell he spoke,
Fixing his eye on redneck and geek,
        The strong, the weak and the woke.

He thundered, "You'll all end up in hell
        If you don't repent,
Spending the hereafter with the devil
        And live with eternal torment."

'Twas a favorite part of his homily,
        This quoting of the holy writ,
Telling people, "You're going to hell ..."
        And getting away with it.

The church bell rang the quarter-hour,
        Then tolled three more times;
Yet on he went – the parishioners
        Oblivious to the chimes.

David Colpitts

His oratory thundered in their ears
      As they sat on rock-hard pews;
Bolt upright and wide-awake,
      'Twas impossible to snooze.

His skills of oration were renowned;
      He spoke with compelling conviction;
No nodding off up to the end
      When he gave the benediction.

He shook their hands as out they filed
      Cloaked in their inspired daze;
Said they took his words to heart,
      Impelled to mend their ways.

Even Fiendish Felix was deeply moved;
      From sin he vowed to abstain;
He said, "You weren't like the wood on the window;
      You were like a real *peign*."

Peign?

Peign? Peign? – That's not a word;
      What meaning could be construed?
Did Fiendish Felix mean pain? or pane?
      So agonized Preacher Jude.

Strip Your Butt

I nominate "strip your butt" as slogan of the year. I'm not talking about mooning here. Nor about a recruiting ad for a colony of Hairy Harry's Nudity Nuts. I'm talking about a cigarette butt.

Yesterday, a smoker ambled past my window and flicked the last 17 percent of his still-glowing cigarette onto my driveway. This was a flick of skill, honed over years of practice. Smokers practice flicking like baseball players practice spitting. It has to look cool and they don't want to miss. The butt flew through the air, tumbled like a stick thrown for a dog, and landed with a skip and a roll. The smoker watched with an appraising eye before continuing his stroll, a nicotine-induced serenity gracing his brow.

Nicotine-induced serenity gracing his brow indeed! What I should have seen was butt-throwing guilt vexing his brow. He had just committed the crime of littering. Signs everywhere tell us not to litter. Doubt not that he had littered. But did he show any embarrassment? Any remorse? Any shame? No, his brow was graced by serenity, not guilt.

Yesterday I picked up four butts from my yard. If I hadn't disposed of them, they might have remained there for a decade or more before decomposing. Four butts of how many billions thrown away every year? Do I risk more than a crick in the back from picking up butts? Could I get rabies, for example? Hepatitis Q? A sexually transmitted disease without the body-to-body exchange of not-so-vital bodily fluids? I await the ensuing medical research with bated breath, but I do know I can get disgust, revulsion and hatred, all from one little butt.

What, you ask, is a smoker to do, stuff it into his pocket? The answer is – Yes. Not a live, glowing cigarette, of course. A portable ashtray is the best answer. But even without a portable ashtray, there is no need to litter.

Here's the technique for all you smokers. When you have finished smoking your cigarette, stub it out, on your shoe if necessary, or slide your fingers forward from the filter towards the lighted end and squeeze – the burning tobacco end will drop off. Make sure it drops off on a non-inflammable surface and that it is out. Next, roll the cigarette between your fingers. The loose tobacco will scatter in the breeze, invisible. Then tear off the remaining bit of paper, roll it into a small ball and swallow it. Or, if you are allergic to paper – and just to keep your skills intact – flick it away. It's so small nobody bigger than an ant will ever see it and the paper will soon decompose. Finally, slip the ash-free, tobacco-free, guilt-free filter into your pocket for proper disposal later. Voilà – all necessary elements are there – the nicotine-induced serenity of brow, the practiced flick and my litter-free driveway.

This is not a new technique. I learned it years ago as a young lad in the army. We all smoked then, of course, before we learned that cancer cures smoking. Sometimes we would roll our own to save a buck or two, but the technique is the same; you just don't have a filter to take home. The sergeant called it "field stripping." Littering wasn't his only concern. Enemy intelligence was also a key factor. Apparently, enemy intelligence could determine an outfit's nationality by the butts they left. Enemy intelligence wanted to know when the troops of one nation replaced the troops of another. Enemy intelligence knew that Camels weren't from the mid-east and that flinty-eyed Marlborough Men didn't come from Liverpool.

Not only do butt flickers cause litter, but they also cause fires. Some 85 percent of wildfires are human caused. Unextinguished cigarette butts is one of those causes, and a major one. Flick a glowing butt out a car window, for example, or discard a live butt while walking in the woods and you can torch thousands of acres of forest. Fines for littering in one jurisdiction (Calgary, Alberta) show how serious this is. It's $250 to $500 for improper disposal of a cigarette butt and up to $750 for throwing a butt out a car window.

Flicking a butt thirteen feet takes a lot of skill. Not flicking a butt anywhere takes a little common sense. Field-stripped butts don't cause fires. If it doesn't burn up your fingers, it won't burn down the forest.

You may not care whether someone figures out your nationality when you're strolling along your hometown sidewalk, but you might care about littering, about keeping your area tidy and about fires. And who knows. If others follow these simple steps, it just might reduce the number of butts you have to pick up from your own property. So take a lesson from the sergeant – field strip your butts.

David Colpitts

Career Change – From Star to Politician

The loudspeakers roar, "Heeeeeer's Maaaaayooor SOLLEEE."

Mayor Solley emerges from behind the curtains. He prances on stage with one of his well-rehearsed entry antics, this time a pirouette clockwise followed by a hop forward with outstretched hands and a loud "Ta da." He pauses, then waves to the crowd, saying, "Thank you, thank you."

Solley used to be a late-night talk show host. After one of his many standard juvenile entry capers, he launches into a short stand-up comedy routine.

"A funny thing happened on my way to the rally tonight. Just outside the gates, I stepped into some doggy do-do. Smelly, messy and gooey. It must have been left there by Doggy Do-Do Dimple Whitt, that other guy who's trying to win this election."

"Boo, shame, shame," says the crowd, or words to that effect.

Solley goes on, "Smelly, messy and gooey – just like his campaign. Can you believe it? He stood on the corner of 7th and 12th in the rain holding up a sign saying 'Vote Dimple Whitt for mayor.'"

"Boo, shame, shame," says the crowd, or words to that effect.

"In the rain. Right in the rain. Can you believe it? No wonder he's all wet."

"Boo, shame, shame," says the crowd, or words to that effect.

"He was standing in the middle of a puddle. Right in the middle of a puddle. Can you believe it? He didn't have the common sense to stand on something. That just shows you – no platform to stand on. None at all."

"Boo, shame, shame," says the crowd, or words to that effect.

"Hey, we've got a great show for you tonight."

"Applause. Applause."

"First is Amazon Amaly, the Star of Amazon. She's a guru of the online sales gig, and she's writing a bestseller on great politicians. Tonight she'll reveal what chapter I'll be in."

"Applause. Applause."

"Then we have basketball star Towerful Powerful, the Third. All great campaigns are endorsed by big sports heroes, and they don't get any bigger than Towerful. He's seven feet, one inch tall. He's been practicing his grammar and learning how to put together several sentences in a row so he can advertise something other than athletic shoes. He never got around to learning anything but basketball in all his years in college."

"Applause. Applause."

"And finally, the guy with the golden gab, Gary Gallygog, who is going to tell you all about our exciting fundraising campaign, like the 'Make Solley Mayor Again' temporary tattoos guaranteed to stay on your forehead to election day, yours for just $5.00."

"Applause. Applause."

"And he'll be selling tickets for the big "Break Bread with Solley Campaign Breakfast," normally $100 a head but for today only, Today Only! you can get one for the discounted price of $95.99. Did I say today only? He's promised lots of different breads for the Break Bread With Solley Breakfast, and even some buns, certified gourmet buns, like hot dog, hamburger and sticky. For those of you worried about adding on extra pounds at an all-the-bread-you-can-eat break-bread breakfast, we will be sure to have some bread with dietary fiber. And for those of you who are feeling poor, we'll have some with enriched flour."

"Applause. Applause."

***

Meanwhile, at the other end of town, Jane Turnalheads is waiting for former star baseball player and hall-of-famer-turned-politician John Whitt as he steps out of a puddle of water. He gives a high five to one of his supporters, a low five to another, and attempts a chest bump with a third. It fails, his chest having dropped to his navel.

He invites several supporters to join him as he begins his familiar sports hero cavort. He stamps his left foot three times, his right foot three times, puts his hands to his ears, pivots left, pivots right, thumps his chest with both hands, just as he used to do on TV, then points to the sky. The sky ignores him.

Ms. Turnalheads manages to get his attention. "Mr. Whitt, you are running for mayor ..."

"Just call me Dimple."

"That's an unusual name. Why are you called Dimple?"

"It's when I spit. Ya can't make it big unless ya can spit. But ya gotta do it casual like, no scrunching up your face or nothin'. It's just when I do it, my dimples pop out, so Crackerjake Fake-the-

Snake, he's my old coach, started calling me Dimple and it stuck. That's with a 'd,' not an 's,' right?"

"You are running for mayor. Why?"

"It's like the championship, the pennant. It's there. Ya gotta give it yer best shot."

"You are considered by many to be the underdog. How does that affect your campaign?"

"We'll stick to the game plan. We've got a great team. Strong support down the middle, plenty of bench strength, power at the plate."

A fuzzy mascot comes into view, puts its arms around Dimple's shoulder and waves a sign saying,

Vote Wittily

Vote Whitt

"Say, how do you like my mascot? Just like what all the baseball teams have."

"It looks like one of those bears from the toilet paper ads."

"Yeah, it shows I'm here to beat the crap out of that Solley guy. Get it? Clever, eh? And clean up the mess he's making."

"Fundraising is an issue in this election. Your opponent has raised twice as much as you have. Do you have a plan to increase your war chest?"

"I got sponsors. All I have to do is wear clothes with some logo and the company sends money. Like, when you stand in some water to prove the boots are waterproof, you get double."

"You sure have a lot of sponsors. Your shirt looks like one worn by racing car drivers, with all those company logos."

"It's hard to find more space. I'll have to start overlapping. I've got enough glue for five more patches."

"The logo on your hat has something I don't recognize."

"It's for marijuana."

"It is wise to advertise something so controversial?"

"They give lots of money and free samples for my next rally. Besides, my base likes it. My first base, my second base and my third base. And home plate. It's a good pitch. Like a fastball. Right on the lower right corner with a bit of a jump."

"Going for marijuana fits in with your glasses."

"My glasses?"

"Yes – they're progressive lenses."

Dimple turns his head and spits, a spit of elegance, timing and unerring accuracy, honed over decades of spitting through a catcher's mask and not a few years of trial, error and gooey face masks.

Ms. Turnalheads watches its trajectory. "I see you haven't lost any of your baseball skills."

"Nope, I still got it."

Dimple scratches, the way all baseball players scratch. The TV camera turns away. Ms. Turnalheads turns away. Flies buzz.

Ms. Turnalheads pauses, then says, "Tell me about your platform."

"We've come to play. We're on the final stretch. We'll keep playing our game, get confidence, come up big, then give'er 110 percent. Our focus is there to hang in tough and get'er done."

"Yes, certainly unique among politicians. Is there anything else you'd like to add?"

"Yes, I'm Dimple Whitt and I approve this message."

"Thank you, Mr. Whitt."

"You betcha."

Meeting a Bear – Lessons Learned

Remember that song "The Teddy Bear's Picnic?" It starts, "If you go down to the woods today, you're sure of a big surprise." So there you are, hiking serenely along a quiet mountain trail, you come around a corner and see a big surprise in the form of a grizzly bear ahead of you. Grizzly, as in "not a teddy bear." Yep, your hike has just become de-serene-itized (if that is not a word, it should be).

There was no doubt about it – it was a grizz, with the characteristic hump and smallish ears. It was small as grizzlies go. Still, it was bigger, tougher, and – I hoped – not as hungry as I was.

Up until that time, I had enjoyed my hike in the Rocky Mountains in Banff National Park, wandering along a trail above Lake Minnewanka. Down a steep slope to my left was the lake. Up a steep slope to my right was a ridge running toward Mount Aylmer. Ahead was my car, and between my car and me was the bear. The bear wasn't far away – perhaps 60 yards. It was calmly going about its business, poking around in the bushes close beside the trail.

I knew exactly what to do. I took out my bear spray. Bear spray is a concentrated pepper spray. It comes in an aerosol can with extra oomph to be able to propel the spray away from the user. It is said to ward off bear attacks 95 percent of the time if used correctly. That means waiting until the bear is close. Really close, like 18 feet, which is its maximum effective range. I have heard that bears have a strong case of halitosis. I didn't want to find out.

Next, they say to let the bear know you are there by shouting and waving. I shouted and waved. An ardent Montreal Canadiens hockey fan could not have been more proud of me.

The bear wasn't a Montreal Canadiens fan. It continued to ignore me. Maybe I should have shouted like a New York Yankees fan, but I wasn't thinking along those lines. So I shouted some more. The bear continued to poke about the bushes.

That was my first lesson – some bears don't like the Canadiens. Next time maybe I'll try shouting like a Chicago Bears fan or a Boston Bruins fan or even a Chicago Cubs fan. Be careful though. You don't want to give the bear ideas, so be sure not to shout like an angel, as per the Los Angeles Angels or a devil, like the New Jersey Devils.

I decided to backtrack a hundred yards or so, back behind a corner and down a small dip in the path, and wait out of sight of the bear. I didn't have to wait long. Soon after, the bear came ambling along the path. It stopped when it saw me, and like before, poked about the bushes on the side of the trail.

The books suggest that if you back off a ways and wait for perhaps 20 minutes, the bear will move off the path and you can proceed. I shouted again, hollered even, and again moved back down the trail and out of sight, planning on waiting for a while. A few minutes later, the bear appeared again. Scratch that strategy and add a second lesson – bears don't play by the book.

The book also says there have been no known instances where bears have attacked a group of four or more people. I had seen some mountain bikers earlier in the day. They were still behind

David Colpitts

me, so I decided to walk back until I came to some more people. Maybe the bear knew about that chapter.

It was an uneasy walk, needless to say. It's tough walking with head swiveled behind, careful not to trip over roots or stones, holding bear spray in one hand, one hiking pole in the other, and wondering why I hadn't been given a third hand for the other hiking pole. Plus going uncomfortably fast.

The lake glittered in the afternoon sun, the light reflected off the snow on Mount Inglismaldie on the other side of the lake, the slight breeze rustled the leaves on the bushes, the trees dappling the forest path with kaleidoscopic patterns of sun and shade. And I didn't care. The scenery and beauty of the mountains were a part of my trip earlier in the morning. Now all went unnoticed.

How much danger was I in? I didn't know. The last time a person had been killed by a grizzly in Banff National Park was in 1980. It's famous and they're still talking about it. That's not how I want to become famous. I had never expected to meet my demise in a nasty bear encounter. Do you know these prepaid funerals? After a bear encounter of the fatal kind, I might never get to use that down payment on an open casket. Bummer.

I retraced my steps perhaps a mile and a half before I saw anyone else, two cyclists, young women taking a break after a long uphill ride and heading in my direction. They were standing on the trail, bikes close by, while they ate some trail mix. I told them about the bear and asked if I could go forward with them after their break because of the bear. They agreed.

Four or five minutes later, just as we were getting ready to proceed, we saw the bear coming toward us on the trail, ambling along as before. It stopped when it saw us and again became interested in the bushes nearby.

What to do? They both had bear spray and they took their canisters out. They didn't know how to use it. This was no time to read directions, but a quick lesson on how to remove the safety clip, point the nozzle in the right direction, and wait until the bear was close before depressing the lever was essential. The bear was very accommodating – it stayed where it was, waiting for the lesson to finish while being immensely interested in the undergrowth by the path.

The downward slope on the lakeside of the trail here was not too steep. We decided to drag the bikes off the trail and wait there to see what would happen. We managed to haul them down about 20 yards and waited, bear spray at the ready.

We didn't have long to wait. Shortly after we moved off, the bear continued along the path. It walked past where we were waiting, looking neither right nor left, and on until out of sight.

And so the final lesson: if the bear wants the trail, let him have it. Oh yes, and make sure you know how to use your bear spray before you leave home.

David Colpitts

Ask Your Doctor About . . .

TV ads for prescription drugs are ubiquitous in America, a surprise to me on my first winter in Arizona. Why? Because the United States is one of only two countries (the other being New Zealand) that permits pharmaceutical companies to advertise drugs directly to consumers on television. And how could they not awaken latent hypochondriac tendencies?

I'm making a list of questions to ask my doctor, starting with those helpful suggestions on TV. Ads have given me enough questions to drive my health insurance costs from atrocious to abominable and my doctor from amiable to belligerent.

These are the ads that want me to buy some medicine. They can't urge me to pop over to the drugstore and pick it up right then and there. No, these are prescription medicines, which must be prescribed by a medical professional. All they want me to do is to pop over to my doctor right then and there – Right Then and There – to ask if some medicine is right for me.

I'm wondering if the medicine PPP Eradicator is right for me. That's the new highly effective treatment for purple/putrid pimples. I don't know if the pimples I have are actually purple/putrid pimples but the ad says I'm supposed to ask if the drug is right for me. It might not be right for me, but I better check, just to make sure.

The ad says it's not for everybody. I'm sure that includes those with a phobia for side effects. Side effects are to the medical profession what collateral damage is to the military and a boo-boo is to your mummy. The narrator in the ad reads the side effects as quickly as he can in his small print voice. He warns me that if I suddenly experience a biggie, I'm to contact my doctor immediately. I'll keep my undertaker's phone number handy too, just in case.

Oh yes, I better tell my doctor about all my other ailments, the pills I am already taking and any allergies I have. This I'm supposed to tell my doctor. Doesn't she already know? After all, she's my doctor and she was the one who told me to take those pills in the first place.

That ad for high cholesterol is on my list, too. Could it be right for me? Yes, of course, it's available by prescription only and has a list of side effects long enough to set a smarmy swarm of solicitors salivating.

And then there's a pill to protect me against heart attack or stroke, a pill for diabetes and another one for Alzheimer's. And joy of joys, there is a pill for the heartburn that you get from watching all these ads. They're all on my list.

Do you want to read the fine print instead of hearing it? You can check it out in a magazine. The TV guy says, "See our ad in such and such magazine." Just what I want: an ad advertising an ad. Worse, it's not the same magazine. No, each pill advertises in a different publication. That explains why pharmacies have more space for magazines than for pills.

I found seven "Is it right for me" questions sandwiched within one hour of local and national news. Ok, so I clicked between channels, but not a lot. I just applied typical male pattern surfing. Imagine how many questions I might have had if I had watched longer.

The drug ads have the same format. They show happy people who, seemingly, have been helped after they asked their doctor the right question. Sometimes the ad throws in a puppy or a young child beside the patient. This ups the warm fuzzies factor. They don't say what the pills do – they just say it is "for" high cholesterol or "for" ED. Clearly, warm fuzzies are better than facts.

The format is the same. Only the name of the drug is changed. Why are we bombarded with so many? Because they must work. And if they work for pills, wouldn't they work for cars? or beer?

It's bound to happen. We'll see a man firm of chin and steely of eye, his dark hair streaked gray at the temples, his shirt open at the neck to reveal a necklace with more gold than a star Olympic swimmer. He's sitting in a fire-engine-red convertible with a young woman with blonde hair that might be natural and a cleavage that couldn't possibly be. Both are smiling. She looks into his eyes. He looks into her eyes. Male viewers don't look at her eyes. Female viewers gag. They drive off into the sunset, scooting along an unnatural, potholes-free road with clear white lines and beautiful scenery, while the fine print says "Closed course, professional driver. If you drink, don't drive; people cause accidents."

Then the voice-over: Ask your automotive professional if a Lightning Bolt convertible is right for you. It is not for everyone, including those who live in the Arctic, carry golf clubs in the trunk or are allergic to airbags. Available by massive financing outlays only. Side effects include speeding tickets, windburn, bad hair and an irascible wife. See our ad in Racy Driver Magazine.

I'm Florally Challenged

And beer ads. The setting is inside a pub. The guy is good-looking, but not rich like the man in the car ad. The blonde is the same one from the car ad. If she wants to be rich, she should hang around with the guy in the other ad. Above the bar a sign flashes neon purple. People crowd the dance floor. Some talk. Some dance. Our Hero and Heroine are at opposite ends of the dance floor as the camera frames them, holding bottles of Guzzel Beer. He looks at her. She looks at him. He focuses on her beer – on her BEER, for Pete's sake. She has a figure that would put an hourglass to shame and a smile that Pepsodent would pay a million for, and he only looks at her beer. Because she drinks Guzzel, he decides she's the girl for him. Makes you wonder about guys who drink beer, doesn't it?

Then the voice-over: Ask your alcohol beverage professional if Guzzel is right for you. It is not for everyone, including those who are underage, don't like to get up to pee at 3:00 am or prefer their suds in soap. Available by bottle only. Side effects include aches where common sense should have been the night before, fuzzy tongue, bad breath and an irascible wife. See our ad in Drink Safe and Cultivate Bad Grammar Magazine.

Then the small print at the bottom of the screen that you can't read after guzzling your Guzzel: "Open bar, professional model. If you drink, don't park; accidents cause people."

Yep, I have plenty to ask my doctor, and if I watch any more TV ads, the question about heartburn will be right at the top of my list.

Will my doctor wonder about all these questions? Perhaps. But then, I'll have to assure her that just because I'm a hypochondriac, it doesn't mean I'm not sick.

The Last Word

Thank you for letting me share my stories and poems with you. It's been fun to put together what is admittedly a diverse collection of fiction and non-fiction gathered over several decades. Some of the articles have been published in newspapers or magazines. Many have been read aloud to writers' groups.

I am well on my way to having enough material for a second volume similarly composed, which I hope to publish in the coming year.

I am not a prolific writer, writing when the muse strikes and time permits. Other activities – hiking, backpacking, music, travel, volunteering – intrude. The stories also reflect my world. Older, retired, and alternating between the two locales of an Alberta summer and an Arizona winter. Someday I may learn more about the latest gismos and get involved in social media. It would open a new universe of topics for me. But it's hard to keep up with the latest trends. Actually, it's been hard ever since Elvis departed.

Besides the stories, I included two poems. One, "The Visit," was recently published in *The Doggerelist,* one of two short collections of humorous poems available from PageMasterPublishing. ca/Shop or from me at the email address below.

Some thank-you's are in order. First, my wife, Wendy, who supports and encourages my writing. Bonnie Papenfuss, author of two highly entertaining books available on Amazon, kindly scrutinized the manuscript for grammatical and punctuation errors and found far more than I thought even existed; any mis-corrections are my fault. And finally, my friends in writing groups in both Alberta and Arizona who taught me much and encouraged me to publish my stories and poems.

David Colpitts
dwcpublishers@gmail.com

David Colpitts at the PageMaster Store
https://pagemasterpublishing.ca/by/david-colpitts/

To order more copies of this book, find books by other Canadian authors,
or make inquiries about publishing your own book, contact PageMaster at:

PageMaster Publication Services Inc.
11340-120 Street, Edmonton, AB T5G 0W5
books@pagemaster.ca
780-425-9303

catalogue and e-commerce store
PageMasterPublishing.ca/Shop

Also available through Amazon, and other book retailers

About the Author

David Colpitts writes essays, short stories and doggerel. Some of it is fiction. He used to work for the Government of the Northwest Territories in Yellowknife, writing position papers, briefing notes and minister's statements. Some of it was non-fiction spin. These days, he spends most of his time hiking, backpacking, travelling, volunteering and procrastinating. Oh, and practising his harmonica in the forlorn hope that someday someone – anyone – might recognize a tune. He winters in Arizona and lives in Canmore with his wife and his cedar-strip canoe. All three have retired.

www.ingramcontent.com/pod-product-compliance
Lightning Source LLC
Chambersburg PA
CBHW070639130626
46555CB00006B/2623